WITNESS

Alex Wheatle

First published in Great Britain in 2022 by
Serpent's Tail,
an imprint of Profile Books Ltd
29 Cloth Fair
London
EC1A 7JQ
www.serpentstail.com

1 3 5 7 9 10 8 6 4 2

Printed and bound in Great Britain by
CPI Group (UK) Ltd, Croydon, CR0 4YY

A CIP catalogue record for this book is
available from the British Library.

ISBN 978 1 78816 834 2
eISBN 978 1 78283 866 1

Chapter One

The School Run

'Mum, I can't find her hat,' I yelled from the hallway.

'Ask her where she took it off,' Mum shouted from her bedroom. 'She doesn't need it anyhow, it's not so cold today.'

Angela stood very still. She stared at her scuffed shoes. They looked a little tight on her. I tried my best to make them look presentable, but we ran out of polish two weeks ago. My little sister looked younger than her seven years. I knelt to try and attract her gaze. She glanced up at me. There was a smudge on one of her cheeks. I licked my finger and caressed it off.

'Can you remember where you took off your hat, Ange?'

For a moment she stared into space. Then she shook her head.

'Wait here,' I said.

I hunted for it in the front room and in the

kitchen at the end of the hallway. Last night's dirty dishes were still in the sink. The cold-water tap dripped like it always had, no matter how tight you turned the handle. The letter on the kitchen table that Angela had taken home from school had yet to be opened. The milk spilt in the corner hadn't been mopped up. No hat anywhere. I checked in the front room again.

There it was. Behind our sofa. I picked it up, shook it and swiped the dust from it. I gave the hat to Angela and she gave me one of her special smiles. I fitted it on to her head and she hugged me tight.

'You better get a move on,' Mum said. 'It's ten to nine.'

'I'm going, Mum.'

'And don't hang around when you drop her off,' Mum warned. 'You don't wanna be late for the taxi to pick you up for the PRU. I don't wanna hear him tooting his bloody horn – it gives me a raging headache.'

It'd been two weeks now. Shouldn't have been me who got excluded from school. Kelleher was the one dropping insults on *me*. I know I should have ignored him, but calling me Captain No-Brands made me switch on him. His cheekbones bruised my knuckles but his left eye wasn't looking too pretty. At least heading to the PRU – that's the pupils referral unit, innit – would get me out of the way of Mum's temper ride. She'd been blistering the inside of my head since I got expelled.

I flicked my fro and checked it in the hallway mirror. Before I closed the front door behind me, I shouted, 'Mum! Don't forget to take your meds!'

'Don't forget to take my what? Cheeky sort! You don't lose that temper of yours. Now get outta here!'

'And try to get out today,' I urged. 'Go for a walk or something.'

'Go for a walk!' Mum repeated. 'I'll give you a bloody walk. Your face will walk into the back of my hand. Now get outta here!'

Felt guilty about not cleaning the flat last night when I knew Mum wasn't at her best.

Angela reached out her left hand. I grabbed it and led her to the lift.

We lived on the ninth floor. Angela was tall enough now to peer over the balcony and see North Crongton in all its grimed-up glory. On a clear day we could make out Crongton Park and the longer slabs of the South Crongton estate. To this day, I had never dropped my size nines on South Crong turf. I wouldn't take my fifteen-year-old North Crongtonian self out there. Not yet.

The cold wind chilled the back of my neck, but I couldn't be bothered to go back for my scarf. Angela's school was a ten-minute walk from our block. There weren't too many parents dropping off their kids in their four-by-fours. The fence was high and the school itself was covered in grim-grey bricks and panels.

We reached the school gates and Angela squeezed my hand. 'Don't lose your temper, Cornell,' she said.

'I won't if you don't lose your hat,' I replied.

'Will Mum be better today?' Angela asked. The hope was fragile in her eyes.

'Yes,' I said. 'Course she will. Now, you go and have a good one.'

'Will Dad come back if she gets better?' she asked.

I took time to answer. 'I reckon so,' I said.

Was I wrong to give her false hope?

'You have a good one too,' she said.

She ran into the playground. I watched her for a long moment as she greeted a friend. I wished I were at her age, where the only things to worry about were missing hats and times tables.

My taxi would be waiting now to take me to the PRU. I wondered what kinda temper zone Ryan Sinclair would be in. He was dramatic yesterday, cussing out the teachers all because his computer didn't work.

I took my time getting back to my ends. Maybe I'd spend the morning at home and clear up a bit. Might spend some time in the park. Bring a tennis ball with me and practise my bowling. I needed to empty my head. Frig the PRU and Ryan's toxic moods. I had a rocket joint in my pocket. I could just smoke the blunt outta that and find a bench to crash on. The sun was blessing the morning, so why not?

Mum was why not. Her bipolar would swing again. She'd lash me with the ghetto side of her tongue. I dropped the park notion.

Chapter Two

The PRU

The cab was waiting for me in the forecourt of our slab. Driver's name was Sheldon. He looked like he didn't have a blessed night. He had two days growth on his chin – maybe three. I climbed into the back seat. Lavender air freshener itched my nostrils.

'You're late,' he said. 'Again.'

I couldn't be bothered to reply.

He dropped me off at my PRU ten minutes later. Sheldon didn't say bye and nor did I. That's how we rolled. One time, he did chat about his son he hardly ever gets to see. Apparently, his ex-wife is the greediest and loudest woman in North Crongton. Not sure about that. There's nuff contenders for that title.

The PRU building used to be a youth club. North Crong gangbusters had decorated the outside walls with their small n inside a big C sign. There was a concrete basketball court out back, but someone had jacked one of the rings and backboards.

Mr Greaves, one of the teaching assistants, pulled hard on his roll-up outside the front entrance. 'Cornell,' he greeted. He checked his watch. 'Late again.'

'And you're ugly again,' I hit back.

Greaves shook his head.

I strolled in. I went through a narrow corridor where the staff had their offices on both sides. I sniffed coffee and stale biscuits. The corridor opened into a small hall where we played five-a-side football if we could be bothered to clear the tables and chairs. The walls were painted in Crongton Park green.

Four blue doors at the far wall led to two classrooms, one kitchen and a panic room where the staff restrained students if they kicked off. Sometimes, kids would go bonkers just so they could go to the panic room and watch a bit of TV or listen to some music. There was a nice comfy sofa in there with fat cushions.

Ryan Sinclair had arrived early for once. He was downloading a bottle of orange fizz in the corner of the hall. Bigger Thomas, who looked more like twenty-five than sixteen, was with him. His beard could've offered a bed for a rat. He swallowed Rolos and didn't chew too much. An afro comb squatted in his wild hair. I couldn't have allowed mine to grow like that.

Patsy Knowles was there too. Her eyelashes were long enough to rake long-jump pits. She had pretty baby-brown eyes and a body that a world of girls would pay good gym time for. Her pink and blue hair looked like the arc of a rainbow. She sat down on a chair and was swiping away on her phone. Her friend, Bootsy, was with her. Bootsy was wearing a black mini leather skirt and fishnet stockings. Her breasts were fighting to get out of her polo-neck sweater. Her hair was styled in ponytails. She was the first I heard speak.

'Are you gonna tell him?' she asked Patsy.

'Nah, too much drama,' Patsy replied.

'It better come from you than someone else,' Bootsy warned.

Patsy looked up from her phone. No one had bothered to greet me.

'Tell me what?' Ryan wanted to know. 'I'm not interested in what happened on some D-class dating show, and I don't give a shit about that new singing show either. Don't hit me with small-time fuckery.'

'It's not fuckery.' Bootsy raised her voice.

Bigger finally noticed me. 'Cornell!' he shouted. 'What's going on, bruv?'

'The usual,' I said. 'Nothing breaking in my world.'

'Nor my world too,' Bigger replied. 'Life is too damn boring these days.'

'You're not wrong,' I said.

Ryan still hadn't greeted me. He gripped Bootsy with his eyes. 'Then if it's not small-time fuckery, what is it?'

Bootsy swapped a look with Patsy.

'It's nothing to get your dick in a twist,' said Patsy.

'Will you stop dodging the puddles on this one!' Ryan raised his tones. 'What the fuck you on about? And my dick is too hard to get in a twist!'

I had to laugh at that one. Patsy kissed her teeth and smiled.

'Maypen Butler,' Bootsy revealed.

'Who's Maypen Butler when he has a wank?' Ryan wanted to know.

'It's not the top story on Sky News,' Patsy shrugged. 'Not important.'

'Who the fuck is Maypen Butler?' Ryan raised his voice another notch.

Silence.

Everyone looked at each other.

'Some kerb slug who hit on me the other day,' admitted Patsy. 'He goes to that other PRU by

Dorset Road estate. There's no drama. I told him to rest his paws and to wipe his drool.'

'But he didn't want to take no for an answer,' added Bootsy. 'He kept pushing it, wouldn't leave Patsy alone. He was slobbering hard.'

'Time, guys!' Mr Mott, our English teacher, shouted across the hall. 'We're doing a bit of reading this morning. Althea and Marcus can join us in the classroom if they turn up.'

Althea and Marcus only attended one day last week. No one saw them at all the week before. We guessed they had finally found a place to fuck each other.

No one protested Mr Mott's lesson plan. Maybe because the book Mr Mott had been reading to us wasn't too boring – Danielle Jawando's *And the Stars Were Burning Brightly*. Even Ryan read a page aloud. He stood up to do so like he was in a Shakespeare play.

'We'll chat about this at break,' said Ryan. 'Not having anyone piss on my territory.'

'I'm not a fucking territory,' snapped Patsy.

We followed Mr Mott into the classroom. Danielle Jawando's book was waiting for us at our desks. Not gonna lie, I loved the story. *Why didn't we read this kinda shit at my secondary?*

Mr Mott read for fifteen minutes. Only Bigger Thomas crashed out at his desk and fell asleep. I guessed he smoked a rocket following his three Shredded Wheat. Mr Mott ignored him.

Following the reading, we had a debate about what it might be like to discover a sibling had lived a life and been through shit that you had no idea about. As usual, Ryan wouldn't let anyone else get a letter in, let alone a word. He kept on repeating that his fam had faced most shit that life could fling at them. He wasn't wrong.

Before our first break, Mr Mott collected all the books and quick-toed to the staff room. Ryan remained in his seat. He was brewing on something.

He turned to Patsy. 'You told this Maypen bruv that you got a man, right?'

Patsy stood up from her chair. 'Ryan, it doesn't matter. Let it go. The shutters have come down on that one.'

'Did you tell him you've got a man!' Ryan raised his voice.

Patsy hesitated. She swapped a glance with Bootsy. Bootsy stared at her Trinidad-flag-coloured nails.

'Sort of,' Patsy finally replied.

'What do you mean sort of?' Ryan wanted to know.

'He said that if she got a man,' Bootsy spoke

11

up, 'he wouldn't be able to service her like he could. He said he knows every nook, cranny and nut to get her engine revving—'

'Bootsy!' Patsy protested.

'That's a massive disrespect,' said Bigger. 'Maypen's chatting about servicing your girl, bruv. Liberties! You can't allow that. You're a Sinclair.'

Ryan closed his eyes for a long second. The classroom fell quiet. Patsy offered Bootsy a vicious eye-pass.

Ryan opened his eyes and head-lit Patsy. 'Did you tell this pawn that your man is Ryan Sinclair?'

Patsy played with her phone again.

'Did you!' Ryan pressed.

'Yeah I did,' Patsy replied. 'He's never heard of you. Not everyone in North Crong has heard of the Sinclair brand. It's not like there's a reality programme about your fam on Netflix.'

'He must be a newbie to our post codes,' said Ryan.

Everyone in my hood knew about the Sinclairs and their dramas. Ryan's older bruv, Cartelle, was serving time for carving some Korean bruv in the Shenk-I-Sheck club. Middle bro, Stanmore, pumped weights in a young offenders institution. He had gored a South

Crong soldier with a sharpened wooden spoon. It wasn't pretty. He was released recently. Now, he had more bicep detail than the Hulk's bigger brother. Their dad, Solomon Sinclair, had lived at Her Majesty's pleasure on and off for more than ten years. For a living he burgled mansions and jacked top-end cars in Monks Orchard, Elmers End and other first-class post codes.

'This Maypen Butler bruv's gonna find out who I am,' said Ryan. 'I'm gonna teach that bro some heavy manners.'

'Ryan, leave it,' said Patsy. 'You don't have to escalate this.'

'Leave it?' Ryan repeated. 'Leave it? If word about this shit's leaked, I'll look like a pussy. My brothers will take the living piss outta me.'

Ryan looked at me. 'Would you leave it, Cornell? What would you do if some kerb slug hit on your girl, eh? Especially if he's not taking no for an answer. Liberties! Would you let that shit slide? What would you do, Cornell?'

'Er, not sure. Never been in that situation.'

'That's cos you're a virgin,' smiled Bigger.

'And how would you know if I'm a virgin?' I snapped. 'And what's being a virgin gotta do with it anyway?'

Bigger shook his head and grinned. He had a thing about virgins.

'Not sure, Cornell?' Ryan spat. 'What do you mean you're not sure? The kerb rat hit on Patsy, and Patsy proper told him she's got a man. But this Maypen Butler's not listening.'

Bigger nodded. 'Yeah,' he agreed. 'The bruv needs to learn some manners.'

'We should step up to the Dorset Road PRU and let Maypen know he can't disrespect my woman like that.'

Patsy looked up again. She angled her eyebrows. 'So, I'm a woman now? The other day I was a bitch. The day before that I was a ho.'

'Of course you're my woman,' said Ryan. 'That's certified. All them names there, just banter. You know that.'

Patsy smiled.

Ryan turned to me again. 'Cornell, are you on this? Brothers keep saying that you're hardcore and road-ready. They told me you beat down that Kelleher bruv like he was a living punch bag. My bruvs would respect that.'

'Yeah, I heard that too,' said Bigger. 'You gave that Kelleher bruv some heavyweight manners.'

'When are you gonna show us that you got our spines?' Ryan asked. 'Aren't we a crew?'

'A crew?' I repeated. He'd never said that before.

'I wanna see you fighting live and direct,' added Bigger.

14

'You're not gonna flake out on me are you, Cornell?' Ryan wanted to know. 'Like a pussy.'

'Miaowww!' mocked Bigger. 'Miaowww!'

'I didn't say no did I,' I said.

But I hadn't said yes either. What was I getting myself into?

'There will be nothing glinting from me,' said Ryan. 'I just want to let it be known that Maypen can't take liberties with my girl.'

'He needs some proper North Crong discipline,' added Bigger.

'Let shit go,' said Patsy. 'I know how you guys escalate shit, and it ends up with some machine bleeping next to someone in a hospital bed. That's how it goes in these ends. Why do you have to delete each other to prove you're a man?'

'It's a minor,' replied Ryan. 'Shanks will be a blank on this mission. I'm just gonna let off a warning bomb.'

Patsy shook her head.

'And, Cornell,' Bigger grinned.

'What?'

'You're still a virgin!'

'Fuck you!'

At dinner break, I smoked my rocket out on the b-ball court. Bigger asked for two tokes but took

15

seven. Mr Greaves looked on. He never said a damn word. Ryan and Patsy smacked tongues, and Bootsy munched on a family packet of barbecue-flavoured crisps. When Ryan went to the toilet, I asked Patsy about the scene she had with Maypen Butler.

'He put his arm around me and tried to kiss me,' she said. 'When I pushed him away, he pulled my arm and pinched my butt. *Don't* tell Ryan that though.'

'So, he's a real prick?' I said.

'An A-class prick and a half,' Patsy agreed. 'Doesn't matter where you go in Crongton, guys just wanna take liberties with girls. It's cos of all that mad sex shit they see on their phones. They think that everyone who's got a vagina will scream a big yay to that fuckery. I'm getting tired of all this heavy macho crap.'

We had maths in the afternoon. I don't remember much of what Miss Johnson taught us. They never told us why Miss Bramley, our ex maths teacher, departed. We all liked her, except Patsy. No one quite knew why Patsy gave Miss Bramley grief, but my guess is that Ryan paid her nuff compliments about her figure and Patsy hated on that. Miss Bramley had long brown curly hair and a curvy backside

16

that fitted neatly into her dark slacks. She always wore white or cream polo-neck sweaters where you could make out the full shape of her breasts. Bigger didn't smoke out in her class.

Before the taxi picked me up, Ryan whispered in my ear. 'I expect you to march with us,' he said. 'I'm thinking of a mission to Dorset Road ends. Maybe tomorrow or the day after. Gonna deal with this Maypen fool. Tell him to shut down his gaze on my girl.'

'I hear you,' I replied. 'If it's just a warning ting then I'm on it.'

'Good,' said Ryan. 'You know that from when you bounce with me, foot soldiers from all over North Crong won't mess with you. My bruvs will respect you too.'

'That wasn't on my agenda,' I said. 'I'm on this cos this Maypen pawn disrespected Patsy.'

Ryan grinned a dangerous grin. 'It won't be boring,' he said.

I stepped into my taxi. Raheem was the driver. He was wearing a Pakistan cricket shirt. 'Good day, Cornell?'

'The usual,' I replied. 'Shit still sliding the same way.'

But it wasn't usual. Ryan had asked me to step on a mission with him. In North Crongton. Where anything could happen. It wasn't like I had much of a choice. If I refused, my life at the PRU would be unbearable. I'd be hearing untold miaowwws. It was bad enough at home having to deal with Mum's bipolar. There was no peace for the beast.

Chapter Three

Times Tables

Some parents didn't mind me standing next to them as we waited for the kids to be freed from school, but others side-eyed me like I was a mad disease. I paid them no mind and flicked out my fro. Raheem puffed on one of those vape things as he waited for me inside his taxi. When Angela spotted me, she skipped towards me. A big-time grin rippled her cheeks. 'What sweet you?' I asked.

'I was top,' she replied.

'Top at what?'

She reached out her hand. I took hold of it and we stepped towards Raheem's ride.

'Seven times tables,' she said. 'I got them all right! Seven times seven is forty-nine, seven times eight is fifty-six, seven times nine is sixty-three, seven times ten is seventy.'

I squeezed her hand, stopped walking and knelt so I could speak to her face to face. 'You're smarter than all of us, Ange. No matter what happens with me, Mum or Dad, you keep going on and be tops at your school, right. Maybe you're the one who can get out of these post codes to somewhere better.'

Angela nodded. 'Aren't you tops at anything in your PRU?' she asked.

I thought about it. 'Maybe at cricket, but we don't play it at my place.'

'Can't you tell them to play it?' she asked.

'Don't think that's gonna happen,' I said. 'No bats or pads at my PRU. No stumps. We haven't got a space of grass big enough to grow a daisy. Cricket's for the top-ranking schools. Even our driver, Raheem, has to drive out of the ends to play in his team.'

The flat was quiet when we got home. The kitchen sink was clear, and the floor had been mopped. The lounge was tidy, and the TV was left on at a low volume. In the room closest to the kitchen, Mum was asleep on top of her bed. I decided not to wake her.

Angela found the remote control and watched a cartoon. 'What are we gonna eat today?' she asked.

Good question.

I checked the fridge. There were two chicken fillet pieces. Not much else.

I could dice it up and stir-fry it with whatever veg I could find. I knew we had a cup of rice left. There was a dribble of cooking oil there too.

I started on the dinner. When the rice was cooked, Mum came into the kitchen. She rubbed the sleep from her eyes. She wore one of Dad's old raggedy T-shirts and baggy tracksuit bottoms.

'Cornell, you're a love,' she said. 'I was just gonna do that.'

'You were sleeping,' I said. 'Didn't wanna wake you up.'

'I'm your mum!' she said. 'I wanna cook you and Ange dinner.'

'You just concentrate on getting better,' I said. 'Maybe in a few weeks' time, Dad can come back home.'

'Not sure if he will,' Mum said. 'I freaked him out the last time.'

'He knows you were sick,' I said. 'He's forgiven you.'

'Has he?'

Ten minutes later, I served dinner. I found some spring onions, a fistful of broccoli and a red pepper, past their best but they went neatly with the stir-fry chicken. Mum pulled Ange to her and gave her a monster hug when she learned about her seven times tables test.

I received a text. It was from Ryan.

Confirming the mission.

Tomorrow afternoon straight after PRU

It's on the warning tip

Gonna tell Maypen about his lack of manners.

He needs to know he can't mess with the Sinclair brand.

I put my phone back into my pocket. I ate two pieces of chicken and a spoonful of rice before my phone buzzed again. It was Ryan once more.

Cornell, DON'T mouse out on me.

I didn't reply until I finished the washing-up.

I have to pick up my liccle sis when I finish the PRU.

Mum was reading Sharna Jackson's *High Rise Mystery* to Angela in bed when Ryan replied to my text.

Why can't your mum pick up your liccle sis for once?

It's her job.

DON'T cluk cluk cluk on me.

Before I had a chance to reply, Mum came into the lounge and switched the TV over to Sky News. She watched in silence for a few minutes before she said, 'It's all miserable isn't it? Doesn't matter where you look, all bloody miserable.'

'It's not all bats and caves, Mum. Dad might be home in a few weeks.'

Mum turned the TV volume down. She gave me one of those poor Cornell looks that I used to get when I was younger.

'We love each other,' she said. 'But we can't live together. If we lived in a house with nothing in it, we'd find a wall to argue about. If not the wall, the ceiling. That's how we are. We're good at making babies, but we scratch each other up the wrong way. And my bipolar doesn't help the situation. I could've killed him the last time.'

'But you didn't.'

'But I might do again if we live together again. It's not gonna happen, Cornell. Try and live with that.'

I couldn't really counter Mum's point. They were having a toxic argument about how much money they should put on the gas card as opposed to buying more groceries. It ended with Mum trying to split Dad's chest with a corkscrew. I had to intervene. Got cut on my arm for my troubles. Dad left that night. Mum cried into the small hours. Ange couldn't sleep and watched the Cartoon Channel until four thirty in the morning.

'Angela needs him home,' I said after a while. 'She needs her dad.'

Mum folded her arms and shook her head. 'Don't try your emotional blackmail on me. Not on your dear old mum. I expect better of you. Angela will be fine.'

'Sorry, Mum.'

'Now, how was your day?' she asked.

'Nothing much to say,' I replied. 'We did a bit of English in the morning and maths in the afternoon.'

'Did you keep your temper in check?' she wanted to know.

'Yeah, it wasn't an issue.'

'Make sure you keep it that way.'

My phone vibrated. I picked it up.

It was Ryan.

I decided not to answer it.

'Aren't you gonna get that?' asked Mum.

'Nah,' I said. 'Just one of my PRU bredrens. It can keep till morning.'

Sometime later, I watched the local news on TV in my room – Mum shared the other bedroom with Ange. Ange shared with me until Dad left.

The feds had made a night-time raid on several addresses in South Crongton. They had recovered shanks of different sizes and shapes. Gangbusters and kerb-boppers were handcuffed and ordered to face a grimy wall. One of them styled a silky-looking dressing gown. Another wore a Barcelona football shirt. They also found two kilos of dragon-hip pills and untold plants of cannabis.

I might've been excluded from school, but at least I wasn't in the dragon pill game. Mum didn't have to fret about that.

I checked my phone. There were three missed calls from Ryan.

Smoking cobras! He wasn't gonna let this go. I could almost hear Bigger screaming his miaowwws at me.

I went to the lounge. Mum was asleep on the sofa. Some ancient black and white film was playing on the TV. A glass of water was on the floor. It was half full.

We really needed a new carpet.

'Mum.'

I shook her shoulder.

'Mum!'

She opened one eye. 'What is it, Cornell? Jesus! Can't a woman rest when her day's done? You haven't said anything about how I cleaned the flat today. Not a flaming word. I scrubbed all the floors and dusted all the corners.'

'You done good today, Mum,' I said. 'Real good. I'll do my bit later.'

'Yeah, I did,' she said. 'And that's why I'm tired. It's my tablets on top of that that makes me woozy all the time. Now, what is it?'

'Can you pick up Ange tomorrow afternoon?'

'Why can't you pick her up?' Mum wanted to know. 'You get taken home in that fancy taxi so why not make use of that. Let Raheem work for his money.'

'Cos I'm gonna play some ball after PRU,' I said. 'A bit of five-a-side.'

'Alright, then. I s'pose you need your exercise. You better remind me in the morning so I don't forget.'

'OK, I will,' I said. 'Go to bed if you're so tired. Sleeping on the sofa doesn't do your back any good.'

'I'm not sleeping yet,' Mum protested. 'I'm watching a film.'

'OK, goodnight, Mum.'

'Goodnight.'

She closed her eyes.

Chapter Four

Dorset Road Ends

The next morning, I dropped off Ange on time. I told her that she'd be picked up by Mum later.

She narrowed her eyes. 'Why aren't you coming to get me?'

'Cos I'm busy after PRU,' I replied.

'But I like going home in a taxi,' she said. 'It makes me feel special. I like waving to my friends when I get in the back seat. It's got that sat nav thing I like looking at. And Raheem gave me a lollipop last week.'

'It's only for one afternoon you'll miss the ride,' I said. 'And you'll look at the sat nav again tomorrow afternoon.'

Angela pulled a face. 'Not fair!'

'Be good,' I said.

'*You* be good,' she repeated. 'And don't lose your temper.'

I was the first to arrive at the PRU. Mr Greaves

was impressed with my prompt arrival, but I didn't stop to chat to him. He pulled on his skinny roll-up, blew smoke out of the corner of his mouth and shook his head. He needed a shave.

The good sense in me was trying to change my mind about Ryan's mission. I was devising an excuse in my head about my mum was sick and I had to collect Ange when Bigger appeared. He had a plastic cup of coffee in one hand and a rocket in the other. He grinned at me and I followed him outside to the b-ball court. His black scarf was wrapped three times around his neck.

'Ready for your big day?' he asked.

'S'pose so,' I replied. 'But it's not my big day, is it?'

'Ryan just wants to scare the brother,' Bigger said.

'Yeah, I know.'

'That's what his older brothers liked to do,' added Bigger. He lit the spliff with a black lighter. His cheeks hollowed as he took a mighty pull. 'Scaring ghetto-folk. The Sinclairs get a buzz from that.'

'Yeah, I guess everyone's got their own kicks of entertainment.'

'And Ryan will get ratings from his bruvs for laying down the frights on this Maypen pawn.'

'I s'pose so,' I said.

We did IT in the morning ... or we were meant to. Bootsy and Patsy checked out Twitter and what the Kardashians were up to, Bigger watched a UFC fight and only Ryan and I worked on how to build a website. It was interesting. I thought maybe I could build a website about cricket. Ryan was good at computer stuff. I'd give him top ratings at a lot of things.

At lunchtime, we all stayed in the classroom. We munched our dog rolls, pizza slices and barbecue-flavoured crisps and downloaded our fizzy drinks. As usual, the salad and the fruit didn't get any love. Not sure why they kept serving it.

Ryan finished first. 'What does this Maypen fool look like?' he asked.

'He's long and skinny,' replied Bootsy. 'Beady eyes.'

'This again?' said Patsy. 'I thought you dropped this.'

'Not dropping it,' insisted Ryan. 'My brothers wouldn't have let it go. No way! They wouldn't allow any bruv to disrespect a girl of theirs. I repeat, what does this pawn look like?'

'If you must know,' said Patsy, 'he's got a curly fro, wears a Seattle Seahawks cap and a Nike tracksuit top.'

'I don't want any mistaken identity,' said Ryan.

'Why?' asked Patsy. 'Are you gonna go back to his place and do dragon-hip pills together?'

'Don't get sarky,' said Ryan.

'How much of a walk is it to Dorset Road ends?' asked Bigger.

'About fifteen minutes if your big ass can change gear,' replied Ryan. 'Nobody's taking a taxi this afternoon. We'll leave fifteen minutes early.'

'Will Mr Bromley let us go?' I asked.

'Mr Bromley doesn't have a choice,' said Ryan. 'We just step out *without* any apology. It's what my brothers would do.'

Patsy shook her head. 'I'm not stepping out. You guys do what you wanna do. This isn't gonna impress me much.'

'Can I come?' asked Bootsy. 'I wanna see this drama played out. It's been proper boring this week. Our Netflix account has been suspended and my mum says it's not a priority.'

'No!' shouted Ryan. 'No females on this mission. Go watch BBC when you reach your gates.'

'I can look after myself,' insisted Bootsy. 'And I can film the drama on my phone.'

'Save your batteries,' said Bigger.

'No one's filming shit,' added Ryan.

Bootsy pushed out her lips and cut her eyes.

The afternoon went as slow as a blind slug on a rainy Sunday. In our social lesson, Mrs Wickham tried to get us to talk about our grandparents and what lives they led. Ryan gave us a whole history about the Irish, gypsy communities and some Serbian relatives he had. Where the fuck was Serbia? Not gonna lie though, it was kinda interesting. It suddenly smacked me that I knew so much more about my mum's Welsh background than I did about my dad's Barbadian heritage.

Maybe I should've talked about the Welsh rugby teams Mum has hung up in her bedroom. I could've shown them my pics from our last trip to Swansea. They had a neat sandy beach there. The fish and chips were cheap, the crabs were scary, and Ange loved building sandcastles and splashing water at me.

Patsy didn't want to say anything when it was her turn, and Bootsy spoke a bit about the Trinidad carnival and the sexy costumes the girls wore. We all crowded around her phone to look at the images. Bigger slept in the corner of the class. His snores were loud.

At quarter to three, Ryan checked the clock on

the wall. He stood up. 'Mrs Wickham,' he said. 'No disrespect, your lesson was well interesting and shit, but Bigger, Cornell and me have to slide out.'

'But, but, but,' Mrs Wickham stuttered. 'Can't you wait another ten minutes for the summary and last questions?'

'No, we can't,' said Ryan. 'We have to make movements.'

'Where are you going?' Mrs Wickham wanted to know.

'There's a school football game in Crongton Park,' replied Ryan. 'A few of my bredrens are playing in it. I wanna be there for kick-off.'

'Oh,' said Mrs Wickham. 'We'll pick up tomorrow afternoon where we left it today. Cornell, you haven't said anything yet. We'll start with you if that's OK.'

'OK, Miss,' I replied.

'Bigger!' Ryan raised his tones. 'We're in motion. Slap your ass in gear.'

Bigger stretched his arms and yawned. He picked the matter out of his eyes.

Ryan led Bigger and me out of the classroom. I glanced over my shoulder and watched Patsy shaking her head. I didn't think she was impressed much.

Mr Bromley, Mr Greaves and Mr Mott offered

us long looks as we left the building.

Mr Greaves ran out of his office. 'What about your taxis?' he asked.

'Don't need 'em,' replied Ryan. 'We're watching the football in the park. We do have legs you know. You guys are always telling us to exercise them.'

Mr Greaves checked his watch.

Not gonna lie, as we trekked through the pathways and byways of North Crongton estate, my heart woke up and rang the alarm.

Cornell, it said, you don't have to do this. I could about-turn and head back to base. So what if Bigger miaowwws and calls me a pussy. It's not a biggie. It didn't need three of us anyway. Bigger's crusty enough to scare the acne off any wannabe gangbuster.

Ryan pulled a bottle of water from his backpack. He took a long swig and then looked at me hard. 'Did I tell you about when my bruv, Cartelle, terrorised the kerb-boppers in a South Crong youth club?'

'Er, no,' I said. 'Don't know that one.'

Ryan grinned. 'Some South Crong pawn called Colonel Ribs bragged about giving Cartelle a beat-down. He wasn't lying, but he didn't say it was three against one. Cartelle heard about it on the grime-vine and planned his mission.

Four days later, Cartelle bounced into the South Crong youth club, found Colonel Ribs and mashed him so hard in his sperm bags that he's still pissing in pain. His dick can't go anywhere near a pussy without hollering a big ouch.'

'Yeah,' Bigger nodded. 'Cartelle's a proper legend. He stepped onto South Crong turf on his lonesome. He didn't even have a backpack let alone back-up.'

'You can't mess with my bruvs,' said Ryan. 'They take zero shit. They're not afraid of *anyone*.'

We walked across a kids' adventure playground. There were tyres hanging from ropes, a treehouse, three swings, two slides and a log castle on top of a mound. Youngsters were having big fun. For a moment, I wished I were one of those little kids playing there. They all seemed free from any kinda beef.

Unlike the tower blocks of my ends, the slabs here were mostly five storeys high but thirty flats long.

Dorset Road estate itself had three-storey blocks with blue and black front doors. The brown-painted gas meter cupboards were set into the walls. Someone played samba music from above, but I couldn't quite locate its source. I spotted a postman performing a late delivery.

The heartbeat I felt in my chest now echoed in my throat and in my stomach.

I had come this far. It was ridiculous for me to mouse out now. What would I say? I had to stop fretting. Ryan just wanted to put the fright down on this Maypen bruv.

'This Maypen Butler must've heard of the Sinclair brand by now,' Ryan said. 'Everyone knows us in North Crong. There's not gonna be any drama. If he knows what's good for him, he'll just say sorry and be done. Maybe we can step to the cheesecake factory after?'

'How much further?' Bigger wanted to know.

'Just around the next two corners,' replied Ryan.

I checked the time on my phone.

3.03 pm.

Ryan adjusted the strapping of his backpack. Bigger downloaded half a bottle of water. He wiped his lips. We turned the first corner. Perched on a low wall, a grey-and-white-striped cat watched us. It licked its lips. My heartbeat boomed into another gear.

It was a similar street lined by a long three-storey-high block of flats. A woman cleaning her outside window turned around and looked at us strange. A van driver tried a three-point turn but couldn't quite make it – the road was too narrow. Someone tooted their horn behind him. To our right, a carpenter fitted in a new front door. *Tap, tap, tap*, his hammer went. *Boom, boom, boom*, my heart echoed.

We turned left. Dorset Road. Small terraced houses. Black-and-blue-painted front doors. There was just enough space at the front of the properties for dustbins. There was a bigger building. Brown bricks. Angled roofs. Three floors. Small windows. There was a high gate in front of it. A grey intercom was fixed into the wall beside it. A car park was on the other side of the wall. I didn't think the *Fast and Furious* guys would enjoy driving the rides there.

'That's it,' said Ryan. 'The Dorset Road PRU. We made good time.'

My stride shortened.

'What do we do now?' asked Bigger.

'We wait until this Maypen Butler plants his toes outside,' replied Ryan.

'What if he's stepping with someone?' I wanted to know.

A long pause.

'Don't make a shit of difference to me,' Ryan finally answered. 'We'll wait on the other side of the street.'

We crossed the road.

Someone used a power drill further down the

street. My nerves woke up and ate my spine. A distant police siren piled on to that. I felt the dampness in my armpits and a hot anxiety behind my eyes.

3.09 pm.

The gates opened.

A girl about thirteen years old was the first to emerge. She wore a name-brand tracksuit and pink trainers. She had don't-fuck-with-me eyes. She wore purple lipstick. She listened to something on her phone connected to white earbuds. I took in a deep breath. I tried to hide my tension. Suddenly, my throat dried. I wanted a sip of Ryan's water, but I didn't want to ask in case he guessed I was jumpy. I'd look weak. He might've been fretting too. I glanced at Bigger. He looked up and down the street. I sensed fear in his face. Ryan shuffled his feet.

A boy walked out.

He wasn't tall or slim. He wasn't wearing any hat. No sporting name brands either. I exhaled.

3.14 pm.

Two guys strolled out. One of them wore a Seattle Seahawks cap and a puffy black anorak. He had a confident bop in his stride. Ryan's eyes came alive. 'That's the pawn!' he said. 'That's him.'

He ran across the street. Bigger and I followed him. He stepped in front of Maypen and blocked his way.

Nose to nose. They both lifted their chins.

Ryan was reckless, but I had to give him top ratings for his boldness.

Maypen was more than tall. Six foot and extra. Slim. A few strands of hair manned up his chin. His teeth weren't straight. He had a scar beneath his right jaw. His eyes spoke of bad experiences and a liking for revenge. Long arms swung by his sides. For a short second, I wondered if he played basketball and beat down anyone he had lost to.

Ryan was all hand gestures. 'Listen, pawn,' he said to Maypen. He pointed his finger at his forehead. 'I'm a Sinclair so you better listen keenly. You were disrespectful to my girl the other day. We've been tight for the longest time. Patsy's her name. Can't allow your bad manners, bruv. *Know* your boundaries or otherwise I'll set them for you. Maybe that kinda behaviour is allowed where you grow, but in my post codes you have to learn some discipline.'

From hearing the Sinclair name being mentioned, the guy with Maypen suddenly retreated three steps. He eventually turned around and quick-stepped the other way.

Maypen ran his eyes over Ryan like he was a limping gazelle he was about to maul.

'Who the fuck are you?' Maypen shouted. 'I've never seen your rude self in all my days, and you come blocking my movements?'

'You disrespected my girl.' Ryan raised his tones. 'Sinclairs *never* allow that kind of fuckery.'

I glanced at Maypen. He didn't seem frightened. He bunched his knuckles, took a mad swing and before I knew it, Ryan licked dust from the kerb. He followed it up with a boot in Ryan's spine. At this point, Bigger turned his big self around, and hot-toed down the street. The pavement shook ... or at least I thought it did.

What was I supposed to do?

Ryan's nose leaked blood. He put his hand to his face to try and stem the bleeding.

'Who the fuck are you to distress my day?' Maypen yelled. 'I don't care who you are!'

Maypen was about to aim another kick.

I had to do something.

So I jumped on Maypen's back and sort of bear-hugged him to the ground. 'Alright, bruv,' I said. 'You made your point. Let it go.'

'Get off me! Get the fuck off me!'

Something shiny caught my attention. My left eye. It was momentarily blinded. I blinked. Ryan had bounced back onto his feet. His right hand dipped into his backpack. It emerged with shiny metal. It had a brown handle. The cutting edge was serrated. It was curved. It was forked at the tip. My mum had something similar in her kitchen drawer. She used it to slice fruit loaves, hard dough bread and lemons. As he raised the blade, I sensed the dread in his eyes.

'NOOOOOO!'

Ryan's right arm was raised high. It came down in a blur. When metal separates skin, it makes a strange noise. I can't compare it to anything else I had ever heard. Three times Ryan lifted his right hand. Three times it came down with a sloosh, sloosh, sloosh noise.

For a long moment, I couldn't move.

Shock claimed me.

Time stood still.

Then I saw blood. Creeping, rippling blood. It was very red. Maypen slumped. His eyeballs sort of swirled around. I climbed to my feet. Ryan foot-slapped down the street. He still held the blade in his hand. I fumbled for my phone. I managed to keep hold of it at the third attempt. I gripped it very tight and dialled 999.

'I need an ambulance ... someone's been ... stabbed ... in the back. Be rapid, man!'

The blood kept spilling. Maypen's eyes closed.

'Dorset Road PRU,' I added. 'North Crongton.

I don't know the fucking post code. Outside the PRU ... Pupils referral unit. Make speed!'

What was I supposed to do? Press on the wound. Yes. I saw that once in *Casualty*.

I took off my grey hoodie. I pressed it on the wound between Maypen's shoulder blades. It was deep. He had another cut further down his back, but I concentrated on the graver injury. I felt the warmth of Maypen's blood. It made me flinch. Sliced pizza shot up my throat. Shock was still with me.

Running feet.

Opening doors.

People stared from upstairs windows.

The front gates of the Dorset Road PRU opened again. Two men and a woman came out onto the street. I pushed hard on the cut until they got close. I turned my face away from them.

Would the ambulance come in time?

Would he be pronounced dead on arrival?

Should I spill to the feds?

Mum was gonna go bonkers.

'What happened?' a man asked.

I stood up and dipped my head. I didn't realise it, but my knees were blood-stained. My left hand shook.

'It ... it wasn't me,' I managed. 'I ... I didn't ...'

I met the man's eyes. They accused me. I dropped my hoodie, turned around and ran for my sweet life.

There was no sign of Ryan or Bigger.

Shit! I called for the ambulance. The feds were going to know I was a witness.

Chapter Five

Aftermath

I didn't stop running till I reached my slab. I couldn't tell you if there was a witness to the event or who watched me scorching away.

The lift didn't work.

I climbed the stairs.

Leg muscles screamed.

Sweat dripped down my back.

I looked at my palms.

Blood.

Grime.

Shit. Them forensic bruvs only needed a micro of blood and they could charge you for murder. But it wasn't me.

I turned the key into my front door. I closed it quietly behind me. I walked along the hallway and heard the canned laughter of a TV show. Ange chuckled along with it. I could sniff roasted fish from the kitchen.

I headed to the bathroom. I quietly shut the

door and locked it. I pulled off my T-shirt and threw it in the laundry bag. I stared into the mirror above the sink. Guilt filled my eyes.

What if he died? I'd be up for murder. The least bad scenario was getting charged with assisting a killing. And what for? All because I didn't want Bigger to holler miaowwws at me. What was I gonna tell Mum? Dad? Ange? How would I tell Ange? She looked up to me. Who was gonna take her to school? Who was she gonna sing her times tables to? She'd never be able to ride in Raheem's cab again.

I stripped off my clothes and took a shower. The water bounced off my head. As the liquid whirled around the plug-hole, I noticed a tint of red. Maypen's blood. I shut my eyes. The cinema inside my brain kept on replaying Ryan's knife shanking Maypen. It was in HD.

The blade was bigger now, more like a machete.

I scrubbed myself hard. Very hard. I sat under the shower for longer than fifteen minutes. I couldn't quite tell if I was crying. All I knew was that I'd never felt so bad. I was still, but my heart banged fast and loud.

Somehow, I had to check if he was alive. Yeah, I'd have to make some excuse for Mum and step out to Crongton General. Had to find out.

I dried myself in rapid time, but I couldn't stop sweating. I wrapped my towel around me and made my way to my room. I blasted my armpits with deodorant. I pulled on fresh clothes. It was hard to face the photos of Mum, Dad and Ange that I had taped to the edge of my dressing table mirror.

I couldn't bear to look up at my Lionel Messi posters that covered my walls. He wouldn't have approved.

Maybe I could step out without Mum and Ange noticing.

I pushed open my bedroom door. I checked the hallway. It was clear. I planted my toes into the passage.

'And where do you think you're going?' said Mum, stepping out of the kitchen. 'You've only just got back in. I've roasted some mackerel and steamed some rice.'

'I forgot something,' I said.

'Forgot what?' Mum asked.

'Er … forgot something from the PRU.'

'It's nearly five o'clock,' Mum said. 'Will someone still be there?'

'Yeah … of course.'

Why can't you pick it up in the morning?'

'Cos … cos I need it now.'

Mum stared at me like she wanted to

flame-grill my cheeks. She placed her hands on her hips and angled her head. I gazed at the floor. 'Cornell. Look at me.'

I found it almost impossible to glance up.

'Cornell! I know when you're lying. Look at me!'

I slowly raised my head. I could still see Ryan's knife plunging into Maypen's back. Now it had grown into the size of a Japanese samurai sword.

'Are you gonna tell me the truth?' Mum pushed.

'I did tell you the truth.'

Mum gave me a look. I might as well have tried to sell her Crongton gold.

'Don't make me wait until that fish has gone cold!' Mum snapped. 'The truth!'

Our eyes connected. I preferred the ranting and cursing. I noticed that Ange had turned down the volume of the TV. I sensed she was listening to my and Mum's convo. I felt I had let her down.

'Something happened after school,' I admitted.

'Like what?' Mum asked.

'We ... we didn't play five-a-side.'

'Then what did you do?'

'We ... we didn't go for a walk?'

'I don't wanna hear what you didn't do,' Mum said.

A long pause.

'Ryan ...' I blurted out.

'Ryan Sinclair?' Mum asked. 'Didn't I tell you to be careful about him. Crazy family. All of 'em forever getting into trouble. None of 'em got two bits of sense between 'em. They go in and out of prison like I go in and out of supermarkets.'

'Ryan Sinclair ... he had this beef with this bruv from the Dorset Road PRU.'

'And?' Mum wanted me to explain.

'We went up there. It was just a scare mission. This Dorset Road bruv said something inappropriate to Ryan's girl. I ... I didn't realise Ryan was carrying a blade.'

I noticed the lounge door had been pushed open wider. Ange was definitely listening.

'So, it had nothing to do with you?' Mum raised her voice. 'Let me guess, like a total idiot, you followed Ryan Sinclair. What's a matter with you? It's not your girlfriend.'

'Honestly ... I didn't know it would end up like ...'

'Like what, Cornell? Out with it.'

'The ... the Dorset Road bruv got shanked ... in the back. I called the ambulance. I ... I made sure I did that.'

Mum's stare intensified. 'Shanked?' she repeated. 'You mean knifed?'

I nodded.

'Is the boy OK?'

'I ... I dunno. That's why I wanna—'

'Didn't I tell ya,' Mum talked over me. 'Stay away from the Sinclairs. Didn't I tell you that before you started at that PRU? But what do you do? You go following him around like a fan boy and someone gets knifed. *Typical*. Another family in pain in bloody North Crongton.'

'I ... I didn't know that was gonna happen.'

'He's a Sinclair!' Mum raised her voice. 'What do you bloody expect was gonna happen? He's not gonna take you to the park to look at the daisies. You better not say a word about this. We don't wanna be marked. Maybe no one saw you. God help that boy. I really don't know what's a matter with you kids around here. Isn't it hard enough living around here without stabbing each other? Haven't they got tired of singing hymns at funerals?'

'Mum, I have to find out what happened to him.'

Mum shook her head. 'You called the ambulance. You done the right thing. You don't wanna be making any statements. You don't wanna be seen talking to the police, and you definitely don't wanna be going to court to give evidence.'

'Mum, he ... he might be dead.'

We stared at each other for five seconds. The lounge door creaked. I couldn't take Mum's toxic gaze any more. I dropped my eyes to the floor.

'I'm warning you, Cornell,' Mum said. *'Don't* get involved. Things are bad enough already without grassing on the Sinclairs. That'll create a whole bag of crabs.'

'Who says I was gonna snitch?' I said. 'I just wanna find out if the bruv's OK.'

'It'll be best if you just stayed at home,' Mum said. 'And I don't want that mackerel and rice going to waste.'

'Mum, sorry,' I said. 'I've gotta see how he is.'

Chapter Six

Crongton General

I grabbed another hoodie from the peg in the hallway and opened the front door.

'If I hear you've been blabbing to anyone about this, I'll give you what for,' Mum warned. 'If you grass up Ryan Sinclair, it'll make no difference to the stabbed boy. It won't help him. Only God can save him now. Think of me and Angela. We still must live here and go about our business. I don't want neighbours pointing at me saying she's the mum of the boy who grassed up Ryan Sinclair.'

'I just wanna see if the guy's breathing,' I replied. 'Anything wrong with that?'

I closed the door behind me and pulled on my hoodie. I felt terrible, but I had to check on the shanked bruv.

A spit of rain was in the air. I pulled my hood over my forehead.

'Don't bring those crazy Sinclairs to my door,' Mum yelled from inside.

Even if I stayed, I didn't think I could keep Mum's fish and rice down.

I skipped down the stairs and into the forecourt of our slab. Even if Maypen survived his stabbing there could be a grievous bodily harm charge ... or attempted murder. Someone might've seen me. Though kerb-boppers are always pulling down CCTV cameras, there's still plenty of them around. I left my grey hoodie at the scene. The feds had probably already picked it up. Their forensic people would be examining it. I wondered if Ryan had flung away the blade.

Crongton General was close to the town centre. It was a twenty-minute walk but I reached there in fifteen. By the time I pushed through the entrance, I needed another shower. Sweat collected around my belly-button and down my backside crease.

I marched to casualty reception. The woman behind the counter was sipping a coffee while reading something on a clipboard. Her nails were bitten. She wore a bad cherry-coloured wig.

'Good evening,' I greeted.

She didn't look up.

'Good evening,' I said a little louder.

'How can I help you?' she asked. 'Do you need to see a doctor? Any kind of injury?'

'No, but I've come to find out what happened to a Maypen Butler, a tall bruv. He's about fifteen or sixteen. Brown skin boy.'

Her eyes were still fixed on the clipboard. 'Are you next of kin?' she asked.

'Er ... no. Not really. I don't really know him. Just wanna find out if he's all good. You know. I wanna know if he's been sewn up neatly and patched up. Wanna know if he's up and about.'

'We do not give out personal information.'

'But I need to know.'

She circled something on her clipboard with a biro. Behind me someone had just been wheeled in on a stretcher. He had a white dressing over his left eye. Blood spotted his shirt. He was taken straight through. I sniffed disinfectant from the floor.

'I need to find out.' I raised my voice. 'It's important.'

'May I repeat, it's not policy to give out personal information about any patients.'

I bit my bottom lip and narrowed my eyes at the receptionist. She ignored my hard stare and returned her gaze to the clipboard. What the fuck was so important on her clipboard?

I decided to find a spare seat. Maybe I'd be able to spot Maypen's family members. How would I recognise them? His fam must be tall with don't-tread-on-my-feet eyes. I'd look out for that.

Sitting next to me was a middle-aged guy who I overheard had sliced his thumb at the Crongton biscuit factory. He said hi and something about how he might lose pay. I ignored him. I had bigger worries.

Twenty minutes later, my phone vibrated.

It was Bigger.

I checked his text.

Where r u, he asked.

Better not spill that I'm at Crongton General, I thought.

Out and about, I texted back. *Where r u?*

Bigger didn't reply for five minutes.

At home.

Ryan texted me.

He told me what happened.

Whatever you do, DON'T leak anything to anybody!

I decided to leave the hospital. Tension sweated out of me. I'd head over to Dad's. He'd calm me down. He'd know what to do.

Chapter Seven

Dad's Counsel

Dad lived in a bedsit near the junction of the Crongton circular and Notre Dame Road. It was the grimiest part of North Crong estate. Kerb-boppers called it Murder Square. Dad had seen more police tape than a worker in a Sellotape factory. It was another twenty-minute walk. I sent him a text to tell him I was on my way.

During the week? You don't usually visit during the week? What's up?

I tell you when I land at your gates, I replied.

He called me but I didn't answer.

The traffic was heavy on the Crongton circular. The Notre Dame Road led to Fireclaw Heath. I thought maybe I should carry on trekking to the Heath and find somewhere quiet to rest my bones and forget about everything. Was tempted to download a couple of dragon-hip pills – it'll help me sleep and take me somewhere else. Take me out of this nightmare. Maybe I could ask Bigger – he takes them like a hungry kid inputs Smarties.

But I couldn't. Maypen Butler might be no more. They might have been tying a tag on his big toe. He might be lying in some freezing steel box. A cold shiver flowed through my veins. I closed my eyes and watched Ryan's blade come down once again. Red, very red. Why did I have to see that? Can't remember seeing anything on local news about the trauma that licks kids who have witnessed serious shit on road.

I shook my head.

Dad lived on the third floor. His slab was covered in North Crong gangbuster graffiti and symbols. Satellite dishes covered the block like lumpy, grey acne. I always used the concrete stairs as Dad told me someone recently got jacked in the lifts. Their trainers and phone were taken. *If anyone moves to threaten you*, Dad advised, *just holler as loud as you can.*

The landing on the second floor stank of piss. A half-eaten chicken wing rotted in a corner. Cigarette butts were ground into the dust. I held my nose and moved on.

I slapped Dad's letterbox. He must've been close to the door cos he opened it straight away. We had a moment when we gazed at each other.

His walls were bruised but clean.

'Are you alright?' he asked.

'Just about.'

'What's happened, Cornell?' he asked. 'What is it? You look pale. You're a shade lighter than I last saw you.'

I headed for Dad's little sofa. I crashed on that. The TV was off but the old school radio he had broadcasted the national news. I should've gone for his single bed at the back of his flat – I was exhausted. In body and in mind.

I wanted to shut my eyes but knew that, if I did, I'd see Ryan's blade ripping into Maypen's back.

'Son,' Dad said. 'Are you sure you're OK. Do you want a drink?'

I nodded.

Dad went to his fridge and tossed me a bottle of water. I nearly dropped it. I downloaded half of it in one gulp. I wiped my mouth. I looked around Dad's flat. He had two fresh green plants on his windowsill. He had built a new shelf for his CDs and books. *Wouldn't tell Mum but his place was so much tidier than ours.* I guess he had time to clean up his bedsit – he was made redundant a few months ago from his warehouse job. I wanted to ask him how the job hunt was going, but I thought better of it.

He had Ange's paintings and drawings taped

over his bed. He had a framed pic of me on my first day at North Crongton High resting on his bedside cabinet. If I say so myself, I looked kinda cute in my grey and yellow uniform. The lop-sided afro was all wrong though.

He had a laminated map of Barbados on the wall and a sexy photo of Rihanna.

'Take your time,' said Dad.

I met his eyes and took in a mighty breath. He switched the radio off.

I told him the tale of my day, starting from Ryan sharing stories about his family. I finished with sitting under my shower.

Dad stared at his floor for a few seconds. He gently shook his head. He mumbled something that I couldn't hear. He then looked up.

'You have to tell the police,' he said. 'There's no getting round it. Just tell them what you told me. It'll be alright. Trust me.'

'But Mum—'

'But Mum nothing,' Dad said. 'It's the right thing to do. This Maypen must have a family. If you want, I'll come with you.'

'No, no,' I replied. 'I'll have to let Mum know. I couldn't go to the feds behind her back.'

'I'll go back with you to your mum's and reason with her.'

I thought about it. Mum wasn't the easiest

person in the world to deal with, but I'd rather that than go behind her back to the feds. That'd be a conflict zone.

'OK,' I said. 'Follow me home and we'll tell Mum I'm going to the feds. You better stand by our front door as we drop the news.'

Dad nodded. 'Sounds like a plan.'

Dad pulled on his jacket as I downloaded the rest of my water. He clicked the radio back on and turned up the volume before we left.

Chapter Eight

Facing the Fire

I felt safe walking with him until my phone vibrated again. I guessed it was Mum trying to call me, but it was a text from Bigger.

Just heard.

Maypen dead, bruv.

Can't believe it.

They're reporting it on local radio.

Nuff feds on Dorset Road.

Forensic officers too.

They put up a tent and shit.

Blue and white fed tape being reeled out.

Keep it sealed if you wanna live.

I stopped walking.

'Cornell?' Dad asked. 'What's up?'

Suddenly, I felt dizzy. The shock of Maypen's shanking came back to me worse than ever. My legs felt wobbly, as if my bones had turned into caramel. My head felt heavy. My heart punched my ribcage. *Gotta sit down. Must sit down.*

I dropped my backside onto the pavement. I nearly keeled over. The world seemed unstable. The grey sky looked a lot closer.

'What is it?' Dad asked.

I passed my phone over. He studied the text.

'He's dead,' I said. 'And it's partly my fault. If me and Bigger didn't go with him this might not have ever happened.'

Dad pulled me up and hugged me. *I so needed that.* He held me for a while. Tears fell.

'It's alright, son,' he said. 'We'll get through this. You have truth on your side.'

He patted my head and we started again. I wiped my face. I felt embarrassed for crying in the street.

As we approached my slab, I began to hate the place where I lived. Sick and tired of all the gangbusters and kerb-boppers who always had to show they're more man than you. The playground fights. The look of the shopkeepers as I enter their stores when I want to charge my gas card. The beggars, the hustlers, the dragon-hip pill pushers and their lookouts. The girls who don't look at you cos you're not wearing name-brand garments. Mum trying her best to put a hot meal on our table every day. No cricket team at any of my ex-schools. It's too much. Maybe I should've kept walking to Fireclaw

Heath. At least that way, Mum would only have to provide for one.

I turned the key into my front door. Mum seemed to be waiting for me.

'You're still under my roof, Cornell,' she said. 'You're not a big man yet. As long as you live here, you do what you're told. When I tell ya to stay in, you bloody well stay in!'

She spotted Dad behind me. 'And what are you doing here?' she roared.

'Giving Cornell support,' he replied. 'He's obviously traumatised.'

'He wouldn't be traumatised if he stayed home,' Mum argued. 'He needs to listen to his mum. He's still only fifteen. Give me a minute and I'll traumatise his ears!'

'Rhona,' Dad cut in. 'It's very serious. We just heard that the boy has died. Apparently, it's on local radio.'

Mum's lips moved but nothing came out. For a moment, she stood still in shock. She leaned against the wall. *I had to get another drink.* Dad followed me into the kitchen. I poured a glass of water for myself and for him. Mum came in a few seconds later. We all sat around the kitchen table. Mum bowed her head. I thought I heard a clock ticking, but we didn't own one. Maybe I was hearing the countdown that would bring my PRU ass to a young offenders institution.

It was a few minutes until someone spoke.

'Poor boy,' Mum whispered to herself. 'Yet another one.'

'Where's Ange?' I asked.

'She's in our bedroom,' said Mum. 'I put her to bed soon after you went AWOL. I don't want her to hear any more of this.'

'Nor do I,' I replied.

Dad sucked in a breath. 'Rhona,' he began. 'Cornell *has* to go to the police. They probably have his DNA already with his hoodie. They'll call sooner or later. There's no dodging it.'

Mum stared at the table. Then she shook her head. She spoke slowly and quietly. There was no compromise in her voice. 'Over my dead body.'

'Rhona,' Dad said. 'That boy has a family. They're probably at the hospital right now wondering what the fuck has hit them. And then when it does, they got to call the rest of their family to break the news. Believe me, that's the hardest part.'

'Cornell didn't do it.' Mum raised her voice. 'And he did the right thing. He called an ambulance. He tried to stop the bleeding. What more do they want from him? He doesn't need to be involved any more.'

'It's the right thing to do,' Dad insisted. 'I know what I'm talking about. Whoever killed my brother is still walking the streets. All because *no one* said anything.'

Mum stood up and almost jabbed Dad in the eye. '*Don't* make this about you! That was twenty years ago – Anthony Redrose rest in peace. Let it go.'

Dad slapped the table. He shot up out of his chair. 'It has *everything* to do with me and all of us who live in Crongton – north or south. A boy is dead, Rhona. Doesn't he deserve justice? When will someone who knows what's going on in this estate step up and stand up to this shit? When will this stop?'

Mum folded her arms. She stared at my glass of water. 'And what about the Sinclairs? Do you really think they'll be giving us gummy bears when Cornell gives his evidence in court? Do you? It's alright for you to say, isn't it? *You* don't live with us. Mark my words, we'll be targets. Might as well paint a bullseye on my arse. I'm the one who's gonna stay awake at night. I'll have to take out the windows and replace them with chipboard.'

'That's not fair,' argued Dad.

'That's totally fair!' Mum argued. 'Who's gonna protect us? Even if they lock up all the Sinclairs and their granny, they still have their cronies to do their dirty work. I don't expect much in this life, but I don't wanna be the victim of a drive-by shooting or a kitchen knife in my gut.'

'Maybe the police and the council can arrange new accommodation,' Dad said.

'New accommodation?' Mum repeated. 'Don't make me laugh! I'll have to wait till I'm a hundred and thirty till they offer us a new place. Have you forgotten? I asked for a new flat when I found damp in my room. I went to the council about that and did they move us? No, they bloody didn't. We'll have to have the River Nile flowing through here before they even consider it. And I don't want to move to Murder Square where you are. Angela will have all sorts of nightmares. She'll be stepping over dead bodies and tangled up in police tape on her way home from school.'

'You don't have to over-hype it, Rhona.'

'Am I?'

'Yes, you are!'

'Anyway, with Cornell being a key witness,' Dad said, 'you'll have better luck of getting a flat out of here.'

'He's *not* gonna be a key witness!' insisted Mum. 'There'll be more chance of him playing Elsa from *Frozen* in Angela's school play.'

'Mum, Dad,' I cut in. 'I don't want you two to fall out over this.'

'Then tell your dad to stop dipping his paddles in,' Mum raged. 'He doesn't live here, and he wants to tell us all what to do! I'm not having it.'

Dad kept his voice down, but his veins danced in his neck. 'I'm *not* trying to tell anyone what to do. Let's not forget, a boy has died today. Can't we think of his family and what they're going through.'

Silence.

Mum returned her gaze to the table. Dad stared at the sink.

'I can't imagine ...' Mum said. 'Just awful, absolutely bloody awful. And I don't want to be the next mother grieving. No one should have to bury their own kid.'

'You won't,' said Dad.

'And you can guarantee that, can you?' challenged Mum. 'Are you gonna stop the next crazy boy to knife our son? Are you gonna be his bodyguard, are you? Cos if he goes to the police, he's gonna need one!'

'You're being too dramatic, Rhona.'

'He'll probably need two. Those Sinclairs have their thumbs in everyone's pasties around here.'

I couldn't take any more.

'I'm gonna say goodnight to Ange,' I said.

I made my way to Ange and Mum's room. I heard Mum shutting the kitchen door.

Next to Ange's side of the bed was a small white cabinet with a lamp sitting on it. A yellow light lit Ange's face. She looked so peaceful. She had her arm around a pet dinosaur that I had won for her at the Crongton fair two years ago. She named it Dennis. It was a good day. Ange loved the dodgems and the ghost ride. She did download too much candyfloss on that day though and Mum cussed me out for it. *Do you want your sister to have teeth when she grows up! Her wedding pictures will be a disaster.*

Ange's written work and paintings decorated the walls alongside photos of the Welsh rugby team. A framed black and white photograph of Grandma Evans looked down on us from Mum's side of the bed. I wondered what she would make of it all.

Mum's self-help books, CDs and DVDs filled a shelf and Ange's dolls, books and Scrabble board game occupied another.

I sat down at the foot of the bed. 'Are you asleep?' I asked.

'That's a dumb question,' Ange replied. 'If I was asleep, how would I answer?'

'Hah! You're too smart for me.'

'You're smart too,' Ange said.

'Not really,' I replied.

'Yes, you are!'

'How was your day?' I asked. 'Must've been better than mine.'

Ange sat up in bed and thought about it. She was wearing a baby-blue-coloured nightgown. 'It was Simone's birthday today and I made her a card at lunch,' she said. 'She really liked it. I used the gold and red glitter balls, sticky stars and I used the stencils to write her name.'

'That's so thoughtful of you,' I said.

'Our teacher gave us slices of cake.'

'Hope you didn't eat too much,' I said.

'I didn't,' Ange smiled.

She looked away.

'Hmmmm.'

'And then we had spelling in the afternoon,' Ange said. 'I got all my words right.'

'I've got low ratings in spelling,' I admitted. 'Maybe you can do my writing for me.'

'And maybe you can do my PE for me.'

I laughed and Ange joined in.

It was so good to see her happy.

We composed ourselves and I noticed Ange hugged her dinosaur even tighter. She squashed it against her cheek.

'Are you going to the police?' she asked.

She looked at me as if she were afraid of the answer.

I thought about it. 'I don't know any more,' I replied. 'Mum and Dad are arguing about it. Whatever I do, I can't win.'

'If … if something happens to you,' Ange said, 'I'd want the police to find out who done it. And when they do they can go to jail. They can meet Mr Anderson – that's Simone's dad.'

I didn't know how to respond to that.

'Nothing … nothing's gonna happen to me, Ange.'

I had to tell her that. Didn't want her to start fretting.

'I heard you talking to Mum,' Ange admitted. 'Maybe you won't have to go to court. Maybe Ryan Sinclair will admit to what he's done.'

I gazed at Ange. There was this innocence to her, as if the harsh reality of living in North Crongton hadn't yet tainted her. I wished she could remain seven for ever. Seven-year-olds didn't have to worry about being shanked – well, not as much as fifteen-year-olds.

'I don't think he'll admit to it,' I said. 'Bruvs like that like to be wrong and strong.'

'You never know,' Ange replied. 'He might do. Then you'll be alright. And Mum will be able to sleep at night.'

I smiled at her optimism. 'Whatever happens, Ange, you keep getting good marks at school. In maths, spelling and everything else. Make good friends, friends who wanna get top ratings in their tests like you. By the time you leave school, you'll be able to get out of these post codes.'

'I don't wanna get out of these post codes – not without you, Mum and Dad.'

'Maybe we can all get out of here,' I said. 'Go somewhere far. Live in a place where there's no gangbusters, kerb-boppers and where I can play cricket on a decent pitch.'

I wanted to add no Ryan Sinclairs.

'Would I be able to play cricket too?' Ange asked.

'Yeah, of course. You're a good little batter. Gotta work on your bowling though.'

Ange stared at me for a few seconds. I wondered what she was thinking about.

'Are … are the Sinclairs as bad as what people say?' she wanted to know.

I nodded. 'Yeah, they're not gonna start volunteering at the Crongton soup kitchen. Not good people at all. Nuff people on the estate fear them. And they've got a big family. They've got cousins who live on Pluto.'

'Shouldn't someone stand up to them?' Ange suggested. 'My teacher says people should stand up to bullies. And she said you must tell on them if you see them bullying other children.'

Ange's words cut deep. She was right. But what price would be paid by the person who stood up to them?

'It takes a brave person to do that,' I replied. 'Now, go to sleep, and stop listening to big people's conversations.'

Ange laughed and dived under her covers.

I switched off the lamp.

I headed back into the hallway. Mum and Dad had raised their tones. Effing and cursing spat through the thin gaps between frame and kitchen door.

My phone buzzed.

It was Bigger.

I went into the lounge and closed the door before I answered it.

I kept my voice just above a whisper. 'Yes, Bigger.'

'Ryan wants us to link in Crongton Park at eight thirty.'

'Why?' I asked. 'Isn't it best we stay apart?'

'No,' Bigger said. 'He wants us to get our stories in sync.'

'What do you mean get our stories in sync?'

'He wants us to say we rolled to Crongton Park to play some football.'

'But we didn't,' I said. 'I'm not a snitch but I'm not gonna lie for him. What happened, happened. He's gotta eat his own fried eggs. He's the one who slapped it on the frying pan.'

'We have to stick together,' Bigger said. 'We're crew now – family.'

'We're not family,' I protested. 'We just go to the same PRU. I don't remember you bruvs giving me a badge for my birthday. You didn't chat to me on my first two days at the PRU.'

Silence.

I heard Bigger breathing.

'Cornell,' he started again. 'We're talking about the Sinclairs. Man and boy on road never leak anything on them to the feds. If you do, you're marked. I'm talking about preservation, bruv. Word on road says Ryan's brothers deleted two guys but the feds can't charge 'em. Witnesses have sealed their lips on that one. And it's not just the Sinclairs you have to fret about. It's about their kerb-boppers too. They'd love to rip off a snake's head to go up in the ratings. You know how it runs in these ends.'

'I ain't no snake!' I raised my voice. 'Just don't wanna get involved.'

'You *are* involved, Cornell,' replied Bigger. 'Whether you like it or not. We must get our story on lock cos they might say we're an

71

accessory to murder. So even if you leak out the whole truth, you still might get a long holiday in youth detention before they send you to big man's prison.'

He was right about that. I kept quiet for a while.

'Cornell! Cornell! You still there?'

'Yeah, I'm still here.'

'So what? Are you gonna link us at the park?'

'I dunno.'

'What do you mean you dunno? Don't you like breathing?'

'I'm not scared of the Sinclairs,' I insisted.

I was terrified of the Sinclairs.

'And CCTV is bound to show us making strides to Dorset Road ends,' I said. 'The feds are gonna be scoping that.'

'You don't know that for sure,' Bigger replied. 'Some of those CCTV cameras don't work. I remember Ryan's brother telling me about his court case where the CCTV film couldn't be used. The picture wasn't too clear. I'm saying this for your own good, Cornell, link us at the park. Don't be late and don't let Ryan hate. Think survival. Think of your family.'

'I can't,' I said. 'My dad's here and he's chatting with my mum—'

'You spilled to them?' Bigger wanted to know.

'Er …'

'Did you fart it out or what?'

'They're my parents.'

'Wrong move, Cornell! Even more reason why you should link us in the park.'

'I don't know, Bigger.'

'You have twenty minutes,' Bigger said. 'Meet us by the bridge over the stream near the front entrance. No one can say I didn't warn you. Survival, bruv. It's all about that. No point being brave and shit and weeks later, someone in a white gown in a cold room is tying a label on your big toe.'

He killed the call.

I closed my eyes for a short while, just trying to level my thoughts.

Why the fuck did I ever roll with them to Dorset Road ends?

When I walked into the hallway, I could hear Mum and Dad kicking off. I opened the kitchen door.

'If you really cared about us all you wouldn't have left!' Mum yelled.

'We couldn't go on like we did,' Dad replied.

'You're the father of my kids,' Mum said. 'You don't just walk out. Especially when I'm not well.'

'It wasn't good for the kids to hear us ranting at each other every day,' Dad said. 'Last time, you picked up a knife for God's sake. You went for me. We can't live like that, Rhona.'

'It's not fair that I have to raise them on my own,' said Mum. 'And I was never gonna use the knife. Just tried to make a point.'

'Let Cornell stay with me for a while,' Dad offered. 'It'll give you a break.'

'Over my dead body.' Mum raised her voice. 'Not where you are – North Crongton gang central command. And besides, he has nowhere to sleep.'

'I'll sleep on the couch,' Dad offered.

'Ange's biggest doll can't fit on your couch.'

'I'll buy a fold-up bed.'

'With what?'

'I'll find a way,' Dad said.

'You're not buying a second-hand fold-up bed from one of your dodgy mates.'

'I wasn't thinking of that.'

'And what are you gonna cook for him?' Mum wanted to know. 'Pilchards on toast every day? Last time I was at your flat you had fuck-all in your fridge. You get your food from the corner shop where the corned beef is always out of date. Do you actually know where the supermarket is?'

'Er … Mum, Dad,' I interrupted. 'I'm … I'm gonna lie down. It's been a long day.'

'Yeah, you do that,' Mum said. 'And stay in your room! No going out tonight. Do you hear me?'

'I should take him down to the police station,' Dad said.

'Will you shut up!' Mum shouted. 'You said yourself that the boy is traumatised. Let him catch some rest.'

I closed the kitchen door and made my way to my bedroom. I thought about playing a war game on my Nintendo but changed my mind. I crashed on my bed and stared at the ceiling. I didn't want to close my eyes.

After a short while, I rolled over on to my side. My phone vibrated. I pulled it out of my pocket and stared at the screen. It was Ryan.

Shit on my Sunday shoes. Someone switched on the microwave inside my brain.

Do I answer it? He'd know that I was avoiding him if I didn't pick it up.

I hesitated for a few seconds. If I waited for a bit, maybe he'd kill the call and leave me alone.

Ryan didn't murder the call. My phone now seemed as loud as a brick in a cement mixer. It felt like the walls were shaking.

I answered it.

'Cornell,' Ryan started. 'My main man! I know you're fretting and sweating but trust me, everything's gonna be alright. You know the Bob Marley song, right? *Every little thing, is gonna be alright.* We must get our stories on point. Are you on the same programme for that?'

'Er … it's a mad situation, Ryan,' I managed.

'I thought he was gonna shank me,' Ryan said. 'Didn't you see him move his hand inside his jacket? That's why I pulled my blade. I'm telling you, he was shanked up.'

'No … no, I didn't see that.'

'Anyway,' Ryan cut me off. 'We're gonna say we rolled to Crongton Park.'

'What about CCTV?' I asked.

'Most of those cameras don't work,' Ryan said. 'They *want* people to believe that they do work but they don't. And even when they do work, it's not like HD TV. It's always proper grainy. It's hard for anyone to see clearly. And it was a grey day.'

'I … I wouldn't know.'

'Cornell, link me and Bigger at the park,' Ryan urged. 'Let's get our stories on lock. Once we do that, they can't touch us. I've got a plan A and a plan B.'

'My parents don't want me to head out,' I said.

'What are you?' Ryan asked. His voice was harsh. 'Do you need some spine cream and a back brace? Stop going on like a pussy.'

'I'm not going on like a pussy!' I defended myself.

'Then stop fretting about your parents, set speed and link up with Bigger and me. We're family now. The feds will try to catch us out.'

'We're not family,' I said. 'You're only saying we're family cos you want Bigger and me to save your butt.'

'*You* stepped with me, Cornell!' Ryan raised his tones. 'Remember that! That's intention. I won't be the only one on a serious charge. If we set our stories on lock, we can get through this shit. Stop being a block to my agenda, bruv!'

I thought about Maypen Butler and the kitchen knife that murked him. His agenda was fatally blocked.

'I don't think so, Ryan.'

'What do you mean you don't think so? You know my surname, right?'

I paused. I felt the tension between us even though I couldn't see him. Suddenly, my breathing became heavier. I tried to control it.

'I'm … I'm not linking anyone tonight,' I said.

'Cornell!' Ryan raised his voice. 'Cornell! Don't let me bring heavy manners to you. Don't let me do that. I thought you were on point. You know that if you shout for me, my fam could make you very comfy if you get what

I'm saying. They'll look after you money-wise. No more Alabama fried chicken for you, bruv. You'll be dining in that Italian place Tardelli's in Crongton Broadway. You can take your mum and liccle sis there. *Don't* make me switch on you, bruv. You don't wanna be an—'

'Why did you carry a blade in your backpack?'

'This is Crongton,' replied Ryan. 'I'm a Sinclair so I gotta be prepared for any shit. My bruvs taught me that. And good job I was cos this Maypen peasant was going for his blade.'

'I didn't see that,' I said.

'Cos you weren't looking at him,' Ryan argued. 'I'm telling you, the man was shanked up. It could've been me lying in the mortuary with a tag tied on my toe.'

'I don't think Maypen was carrying,' I replied.

Silence.

I noticed my fingers going red because I gripped the phone too tight.

'Cornell! Cornell!' Ryan shouted. 'Don't forget I know where you live, bruv. I know where your mum shops and I know where your liccle sis goes school. *Don't* let me bring heavy manners to your gates, bruv. We don't wanna hunt you down like an outlaw. I don't wanna round up a posse. *Be* at the park. You got fifteen minutes. Make steps to my agenda.'

Ryan finished the call. I closed my eyes and imagined my shanked body lying on Dorset Road instead of Maypen Butler's. I even heard the sirens.

I had to sit down.

Shit on my slippers.

Mum and Dad were still going at it in the kitchen. I held my head in my hands.

What to do?

Dad had told me many times what had happened to his big brother, Anthony 'Redrose' Campbell. He dated a North Crongton crime lord's half-sister. Mahalia was her name. He was warned off, but he carried on seeing her. I've seen a photo of her. Half South Korean, half Sri Lankan. Proper gorgeous. She looked like Aladdin's girlfriend in the Disney movie. The Korean side of her family ran the Shenk-I-Sheck club in central Crongton. Top-ranking business-looking gangsters. People knew who had shanked Redrose, but no one leaked to the feds. He had a big funeral with his coffin being draped in the Barbadian flag. Dad couldn't get anyone to spill.

I decided to link with Ryan and Bigger. He had threatened Ange. Couldn't allow that. Stand up to bullies, Ange's teacher said. She wasn't wrong.

Chapter Nine

The End Game

I crept into the hallway. In the kitchen, Mum and Dad still banged vocals at each other. I soft-footed to the front door. I opened it and shut it quietly behind me. There was a dose of rain in the air. The breeze was strong enough to make my nostrils itch. The streetlights had come on. I pulled my hoodie over my head and pushed my hands into my jeans pockets. Night pushed out twilight. I started to walk.

7.47 pm.

Crongton Park was a twenty-five minute step.

Kerb-boppers played b-ball in the basketball court in the estate. Every third word was a curse. They were lit by lights that were fixed onto concrete pillars surrounding the astroturf pitch. At the other end of the facility, girls played five-a-side soccer. The referee kept blowing her whistle.

Gangbusters wearing black baseball caps

smoked their rockets and performed their wheelies nearby. One of them yanked a barking Rottweiler dog. Ghetto glam chicks with pink, purple and blue extensions bopped their heads to grime music in parked cars. I'm sure all of them knew the Sinclairs. On my day to day, I was never intimidated by them. They were part of the scenery. *Now, I am.*

Wiping the drizzle from my forehead, I pushed on towards the south of the estate.

My phone vibrated but I refused to answer it. I just need to speak to Ryan. Who was he to threaten my liccle sis? Not tolerating that. Adrenaline pumped through me.

I emerged out of North Crongton estate and reached the terraced streets. The houses here were two up and two down. Only enough space for your bins at the front. Kids who lived here were branded *inbetweeners*. Ryan once said that gangbusters made most dragon-hip sales from inbetweeners.

The rain came down heavier. Puddles appeared in the streets. The wind shook the leaves in the trees. I stepped through the north entrance of Crongton Park. An ugly hound took a piss near the gate. I stopped for a moment.

My heartbeat quaked inside of me. Fear chased my adrenaline. I started again.

I followed the pathway that skirted the pond. It didn't smell too good. Someone nearly knocked me over on their bike. The bridge over the stream was two hundred yards away. It led to a short rise where it offered a view of South Crongton estate, a post code where I had never stepped. A jogger ran past me. On her left arm, she wore one of those heart monitor things. I think I needed one too.

It was difficult to see if anyone was waiting on the bridge in the gathering gloom. My stride shortened.

Did I really want to do this? I'd bring all kinda stresses to Mum's door. And what if Ryan and his fam carried out their threats? I'd be marked for life.

I moved on.

Slowly.

I spotted Bigger first. He was sitting down on the bridge smoking a rocket.

Ryan stood above Bigger. He gestured and pointed. He was doing all the talking. He couldn't keep his feet still.

Couldn't stop feeling that I had a target printed on my forehead.

Had to hold my nerve.

Fifty yards away.

I tried to control my breathing.

Easy, Cornell. Easy.

Thirty steps away.

Ryan turned towards me. 'The pussy reach,' he greeted me.

I said nothing as I approached.

Bigger stood up. He pulled again on his short rocket. He exhaled through his nose. The smoke quickly vanished in the rain. One light flickered on and off in the distance. I heard shouts and cries from the lit tennis courts about two hundred yards away. Why were they playing in the rain?

Ryan looked me up and down. I met his gangbuster gaze. His backpack was strapped to his shoulders. Why was he bringing that?

'So, you finally decided to allow common sense to reach your brain,' Ryan said. 'As I said, the feds can't charge us for shit if we get our stories in sync. Plan A is that we stepped to the park. Plan B is that Maypen went for his blade. And Bigger, you're a witness to that too.'

Bigger nodded. 'I'm on it,' he said.

Preservation.

Ange entered my mind. *I know where your liccle sis goes school.*

I bunched my right fist, levered it from behind my back and right hooked Ryan clean off his feet.

I didn't let him recover. I was on him like an impatient cage fighter. 'Threaten my liccle sis! Threaten my liccle sis! Fuck you! I swear I'll murk your G ass and fling you in the pond if you go anywhere near her!'

I must have hit him with six punches and two kicks.

He rolled away from me, almost dropping into the water. He pulled off his backpack. He took out his blade. It was the same weapon that killed Maypen Butler. It was stained red.

Bigger backed away. 'Ryan! Don't do it,' he shouted.

Ryan didn't hear him. He held the knife in front of him. For a short second, I recalled a moment we all shared in class when we laughed together. Mr Mott had dropped a book on his toes and was trying to hide his pain. It was a sweet moment. Now Ryan wanted to shank me. He had a strange smirk on his lips. I backed away. The blade upped his confidence. It drained mine. This wasn't happening.

I did think of foot-slapping it out of there. Someone had to stand up to bullies. *I know where your liccle sis goes school.*

'This has gone too far,' said Bigger. 'Let's chat about this. We're family.'

Ryan lunged towards me. He made a vertical

slash and then a diagonal one. I felt a burning sensation on my chest. He had sliced me. But it wasn't too deep. Not gonna lie. Every hair on my skin stood to attention. My brain ordered me to set my feet in motion but my legs declined. My eyeballs felt like they were out of their sockets. My cheeks burned. Sweat dampened my neck.

He made another stab and just missed my left shoulder. His momentum caused him to over-balance. With what might I could find, I upper-cutted him to the right of his jaw and smashed him with a left hook to his temple.

He dropped.

The knife loosed from his grip.

I kicked it into the pond.

Plop.

It sank.

Ryan tried to say something, but I couldn't quite make it out.

Blood dribbled out of his mouth.

Moving backwards, I stepped away.

Bigger went to see how Ryan was. By the looks of it, I had sparked him out.

My steps were rapid. I made it out of the park. It was then that I felt a pain from my right hand as well as above my left nipple. I was bleeding. Agony. I tried to flex my fingers. Couldn't do it.

I knew then that I should step to hospital but I had somewhere to go to first.

The town-hall clock chimed in 8.30 pm.

My phone buzzed in my pocket again. I paid it no mind.

I headed towards Crongton High Street. The hard rain bounced off the tip of my nose. I didn't look back. I ran up the steps of the police station. I paused at the glass front doors.

If I entered, I'd be changing the lives of Mum, Ange and maybe Dad too.

I thought of Maypen Butler. I tried to imagine what his parents looked like and what they were feeling. Tried to think what calling their relatives must be like. He might have been disrespectful to Patsy. But he didn't deserve to end up in a mortuary lying on some chilled table.

I stepped up to the counter. There was a policewoman behind it. She wore square glasses. Her uniform was spotless. Her tie was perfect. She looked up at me and smiled. 'How can I help you?'

'I ... I was a witness to something this afternoon,' I said. 'Yeah, I was a witness. Not gonna lie, I saw everything.'

About Quick Reads

"Reading is such an important building block for success"
- Jojo Moyes

Quick Reads are short books written by best-selling authors. They are perfect for regular readers and those who are still to discover the pleasure of reading.

Did you enjoy this Quick Read?
Tell us what you thought by filling in our short survey. Scan the QR code to go directly to the survey or visit
https://bit.ly/QuickReads2022

Turn over to find your next Quick Read...

A special thank you to Jojo Moyes for her generous donation and support of Quick Reads and to **Here Design**.

Quick Reads is part of The Reading Agency, a national charity tackling life's big challenges through the proven power of reading.

www.readingagency.org.uk
@readingagency   #QuickReads

The Reading Agency Ltd. Registered number: 3904882 (England & Wales)
Registered charity number: 1085443 (England & Wales)
Registered Office: 24 Bedford Row, London, WC1R 4EH
The Reading Agency is supported using public funding by Arts Council England.

Supported using public funding by
**ARTS COUNCIL
ENGLAND**

Find your next Quick Read:
the 2022 series

Available to buy in paperback or ebook and
to borrow from your local library.

More from Quick Reads

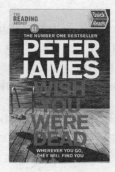

For a complete list of titles and more information
on the authors and their books visit

www.readingagency.org.uk/quickreads

Continue your reading journey

The Reading Agency is here to help keep you
and your family reading:

Challenge yourself to complete six reads
by taking part in **Reading Ahead**
at your local library, college or workplace
readingahead.org.uk

Join **Reading Groups for Everyone** to find a
reading group and discover new books
readinggroups.org.uk

Celebrate reading on **World Book Night**
every year on 23 April
worldbooknight.org

Read with your family as part of the
Summer Reading Challenge
at your local library
summerreadingchallenge.org.uk

For more information, please visit our website:
readingagency.org.uk